BEAR FOR BREAKFAST

Makwa kidji kijebà wìsiniyàn

BEAR FOR BREAKFAST

Makwa kidji kijebà wìsiniyàn

Robert Munsch

Illustrated by
Jay Odjick

Translation by
Joan Commanda Tenasco

Scholastic Canada Ltd.

Toronto New York London Auckland Sydney
Mexico City New Delhi Hong Kong Buenos Aires

Scholastic Canada Ltd.
604 King Street West, Toronto, Ontario M5V 1E1, Canada

Scholastic Inc.
557 Broadway, New York, NY 10012, USA

Scholastic Australia Pty Limited
PO Box 579, Gosford, NSW 2250, Australia

Scholastic New Zealand Limited
Private Bag 94407, Botany, Manukau 2163, New Zealand

Scholastic Children's Books
Euston House, 24 Eversholt Street, London NW1 1DB, UK

www.scholastic.ca

The artwork for this book was drawn digitally on a tablet monitor.
The type is set in Constantia.

Library and Archives Canada Cataloguing in Publication

Munsch, Robert N., 1945-
[Bear for breakfast]
Bear for breakfast = Makwa kidji kijebà wìsiniyàn / Robert
Munsch ; illustrated by Jay Odjick ; translated by Joan Tenasco.

Text in English and Ojibwa.
ISBN 978-1-4431-7511-1 (softcover)

I. Tenasco, Joan, translator II. Odjick, Jay, illustrator
III. Title. IV. Title: Makwa kidji kijebà wìsiniyàn. V. Munsch,
Robert N., 1945- . Bear for breakfast. Algonquin

PS8576.U575B43 2019c   jC813'.54   C2018-905238-4

Photos ©: back cover background: Volykievgenii/Dreamstime.

Translation by Joan Commanda Tenasco

6 5 4 3 2 1   Printed in Canada 114   19 20 21 22 23

MIX
Paper from
responsible sources
FSC® C016245
FSC
www.fsc.org

Donovan and his grandfather looked in the refrigerator.

"There is nothing to eat," said Donovan. "Absolutely nothing to eat."

"There is lots of stuff!" said his mother. "I just went shopping."

Donovan ashidj omishòmisan kì inàbiwag mikwamì atàsowining. "Kà'n kego kanage na ke mìdjiyeng", ikido Donovan. "Màned anòdj kegoshish!" ikidowan ogìn. "Pidjìnag nigì awi kìshpinadjige."

"I want bear for breakfast," said Donovan. "Grandpa told me that he used to eat bear!"

"Well, the grocery store does not have bear," said Donovan's mom. "How about some cereal?"

"I'll go get a bear," said Donovan.

"Right," said his mom. "If you catch one fast, we can still have it for breakfast."

"Niwì amwà makwa kidji kijebà wìsiniyàn", ikido Donovan. "Shòmis nigì wìndamàg amwàgoban makwan!" "Mì sa, adàwewogamig odayàwàsìn makwan", ikidowan Donovan ogìn. "Ànìn tash kijebà mìdjim?" "Nigad awi nànà makwa", ikido Donovan. "Àngemà", ikidowan ogìn. "Kìshhpin tadàtabìn nawadinadj, kidàde amwànàn kijebà wìsining."

4

So Donovan walked down the street looking for a bear.

His feet went *thump, thump, thump, thump, thump* and he yelled, "Bear, bear, bear, bear, bear!"

Behind him he heard something going *trip, trip, trip, trip, trip* and saying in a very high voice, "Kid, kid, kid, kid, kid!"

He turned around and saw an ant. Donovan yelled, "Go away, ant!"

The ant said, *"Aaaaaaaaaahhhhhh!"* and ran away.

Mì tash Donovan mìkanàng kì màdjìkishing andawàbamàdj makwan. Inwewezideshin *thump, thump, thump, thump, thump* ashidj nòndàgoze, "Makwa, makwa, makwa, makwa, makwa." Ishkwayàng onòndàn kego inwene *trip, trip, trip, trip, trip*, wìsakwene, "Kid, kid, kid, kid, kid." Kì kwekigàbawe owàbamàn enigònsan. "Màdjàn, enigòns!" iji nòndàgoze Donovan. Enigòns ikido, *"Aaaaaaaaaaahhhhhh!"* kì màdjìbatò.

6

Donovan kept on walking down the street. His feet went *thump, thump, thump, thump, thump* and he yelled, "Bear, bear, bear, bear, bear!"

After a while he heard something behind him making noises like this: *trip, trip, trip, trip, trip* and saying in a high voice, "Kid, kid, kid, kid, kid!"

He turned around and saw a squirrel. Donovan yelled, "Go away, squirrel!"

The squirrel said, *"Aaaaaaaaahhhhhh!"* and ran away·

Donovan minawàdj kì màdjìkishing mìkanàng. Inwewezideshin *thump, thump, thump, thump, thump* ikido, "Makwa, makwa, makwa, makwa, makwa." Nànàge onòndàn kego ishkwayàng inwene: *trip, trip, trip, trip, trip,* madwe wìsakwe, "Kid, kid, kid, kid, kid." Kì kwekigàbawe owàbamàn adjidamòn. Donovan iji nòndàgoze, "Màdjàn, adjidamò!" Adjidamò ikido, *"Aaaaaaaahhhhh!"* kì màdjìbatò.

So Donovan went into the woods. His feet went *thump, thump, thump, thump, thump* and he kept yelling, "Bear, bear, bear, bear, bear!"

After a while he heard something behind him going *BLAM, BLAM, BLAM, BLAM, BLAM* and saying in a deep voice, **"KID, KID, KID, KID, KID."**

Donovan turned around and there was an enormous bear, big like a school bus.

Donovan looked at it and said, "I'm not scared of you, bear."

Mì tash Donovan kì ijì nòpimìng inwewezideshin *thump, thump, thump, thump, thump*. Àyàndjiwewenin nòndàgoze, "Makwa, makwa, makwa, makwa, makwa!" Nànàge onòdàn kego ishkwayàng inwene *BLAM, BLAM, BLAM, BLAM, BLAM* mangigondàgane ikido, **"KID, KID, KID, KID, KID."** Mì tash Donovan kì kwekigàbawe kichi mindido makwa, mayà igodj kichi kinàmàgo odàbàn. Donovan ogijigàbamàn odinàn "Kà'n kigosizinon, makwa."

The bear opened its big mouth and growled at Donovan: *"Grrrrrrrrrrrrr!"*

Donovan said, "Time to go, time to go!" He tiptoed away: *TIP, TIP, TIP, TIP, TIP.*

And the bear went *TIP, TIP, TIP, TIP, TIP* after him.

"Aaaaaaahhhhhh!" yelled Donovan, and he started to walk: *PAT, PAT, PAT, PAT, PAT.*

And the bear went *PAT, PAT, PAT, PAT, PAT* after him.

Makwa kì mangì pàkidònene ashidj onìkimotawàn Donovanan: *"Grrrrrrrrrrrrr!"* Donovan ikido, "Nimàdjà, nimàdjà!" Kì kàgìmòdàmì kì màdjì: *TIP, TIP, TIP, TIP, TIP.* Kaye wìn makwa kì: *TIP, TIP, TIP, TIP, TIP* onòsinewàn. *"Aaaaaaahhhhhh!"* nòndàgoze Donovan, kì màdjìkishin. *PAT, PAT, PAT, PAT, PAT.* Kaye wìn makwa kì: *PAT, PAT, PAT, PAT, PAT* onòsinewàn.

"Aaaaaaahhhhhh!" yelled
Donovan. He started to run:
WHOMP, WHOMP, WHOMP,
WHOMP, WHOMP.

And the bear ran after him:
WHOMP, WHOMP, WHOMP,
WHOMP, WHOMP.

Donovan ran all the way home and
slammed the door.

"Aaaaaaahhhhhh!" nòndàgoze
Donovan. Kì màdjìbatò: *WHOMP,*
WHOMP, WHOMP, WHOMP, WHOMP
makwa kì màdjìbatò: *WHOMP, WHOMP,*
WHOMP, WHOMP, WHOMP onòsinewàn.
Donovan kì kìwebatò ogì pakiteyàkosidòn
ishkwàndem.

"Yo, Donovan!" said his mom. "Where is your bear?"

"Coming right now!" yelled Donovan, and the bear crashed through the kitchen door.

"Yo Donovan!" ikidowan ogìn. "Àndì ki makom?" "Àjaye tagoshin!" iji nòndàgoze Donovan, makwa pi shàbòndebatò ishkwàndeming wìsini pekisàyàng.

19

Donovan's mom said, "Time to go, time to go!" She tiptoed around the kitchen table: *TIP, TIP, TIP, TIP, TIP.*

And the bear went *TIP, TIP, TIP, TIP, TIP* after her.

"Aaaaaahhhhhh!" yelled Donovan's mom. She started to walk around the kitchen table: *PAT, PAT, PAT, PAT, PAT.*

And the bear went after her: *PAT, PAT, PAT, PAT, PAT.*

Donovan ogìn ikidowan, "Màdjàdà, màdjàdà!" Kì tedibà kàgìmòdàmì wìsiniwàganing: *TIP, TIP, TIP, TIP, TIP.* Kaye wìn makwa kì: *TIP, TIP, TIP, TIP, TIP* onòsinewàn. *"Aaaaaahhhhhh!"* nòndàgozin Donovan ogìn. Kì tedibàwose wìsiniwàganing: *PAT, PAT, PAT, PAT, PAT.* Makwa ogì nòsinewàn: *PAT, PAT, PAT, PAT, PAT.*

"*Aaaaaaahhhhhh!*" yelled Donovan's mom, and she started to run around the kitchen table: *WHOMP, WHOMP, WHOMP, WHOMP, WHOMP.*
    And the bear ran after her: *WHOMP, WHOMP, WHOMP, WHOMP, WHOMP.*

"*Aaaaaaahhhhhh!*" Nòndàgozin Donovan ogìn, kì tedibàbatò wìsiniwàganing: *WHOMP, WHOMP, WHOMP, WHOMP, WHOMP.* Makwa ogì nòsinewàn: *WHOMP, WHOMP, WHOMP, WHOMP, WHOMP.*

22

Just as the bear was going to catch her,
Donovan's grandfather hit it on the head with a
frying pan: *BONNNGGG!*
   The bear yelled, "*OUCH!*" and went out the door.
Donovan's grandfather said,
"There goes breakfast!"

Kedjishk kidji bàmashe makwa nawadinàdj, Donovan omishòmisan ogì pakitendibewàn oshitigwànining màmawe sàsekwàn: **BONNNGGG!** Makwa kì nòndàgoze, "Ouch!" kì ani sàgaham ishwàndeming. Donovan omishòmisan ikidowan, "Mì sa apane kijebà mìdjim!"

25

"Pizza," said Donovan, "does not have big teeth. Let's have pizza for breakfast."

"Tajwegidjìshkiwagizigan," ikido Donovan, "kà'n mangàbidesì. Amwàdà tajwegidjìshkiwagizigan."